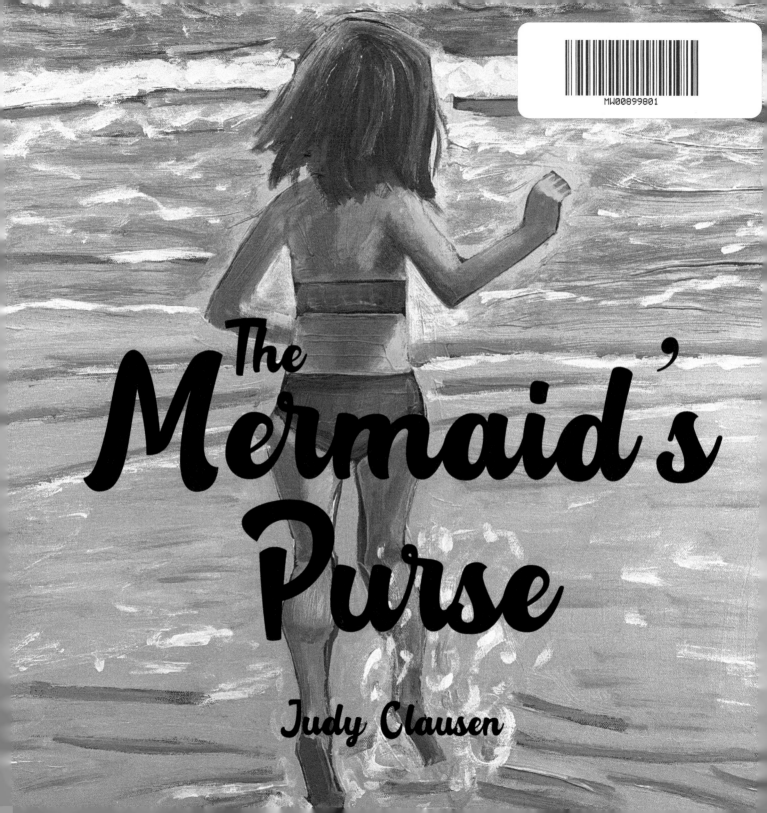

The Mermaid's Purse

Judy Clausen

ISBN:
Hardback: 978-1-952320-40-8
Paperback: 978-1-952320-39-2

The Mermaid's Purse

Copyright © 2020 by Judy Ann Clausen

Yorkshire Publishing
1425 E 41st Pl
Tulsa, OK 74105
www.YorkshirePublishing.com
918.394.2665

Published in the USA

This book belongs to

Amelia and I woke up, ran outside, and climbed the backyard tree in our PJs. We picked oranges and carried them to the kitchen.

2

Hydrangea

As we slurped down fresh squeezed orange juice, we heard, "KNOCK, KNOCK" on the door. I peered through the peephole to find…

State Fruit – Orange

State Beverage – Orange Juice

3

our neighbors, Coral and Henry.

As I creaked open the door, Coral asked, "Marjorie and Amelia, wanna walk to the beach?" Mama said we could go.

So, we wandered out the front door,
down the sidewalk, through the woods,

State Soil –Myakka
Fine Sand

6

State Tree – Sabal Palm

over the dunes,
on the wooden path,
and onto the sand.

Our toenails sparkled like periwinkle shells.

After we built sandcastles, Henry suggested,
"Whaddaya say we hunt for seashells?
Don't take living creatures." So, we
zigzagged the beach, searching for shells.

9

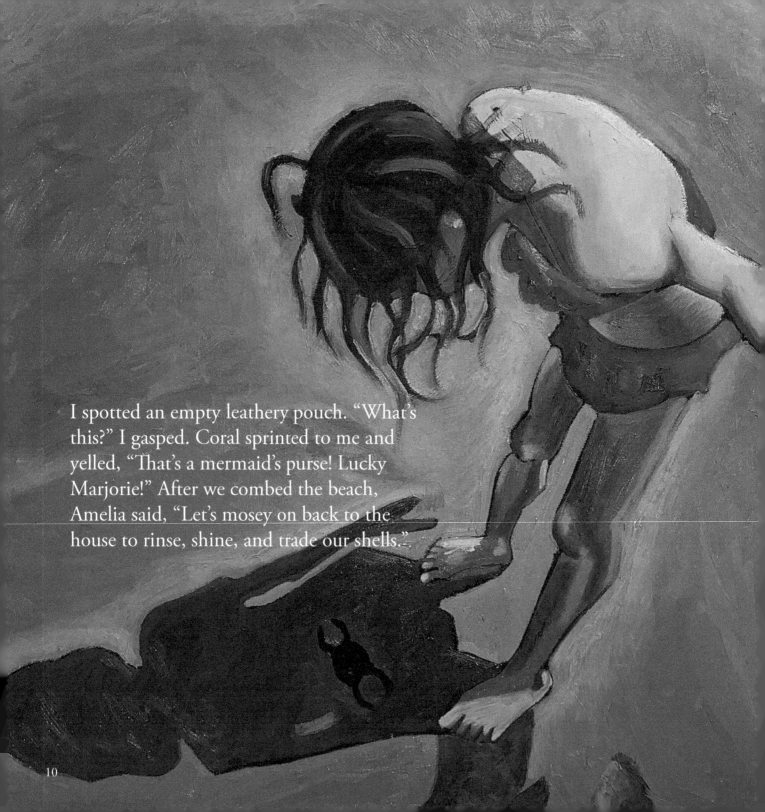

I spotted an empty leathery pouch. "What's this?" I gasped. Coral sprinted to me and yelled, "That's a mermaid's purse! Lucky Marjorie!" After we combed the beach, Amelia said, "Let's mosey on back to the house to rinse, shine, and trade our shells."

10

Spanish Moss

Live Oak

Historic Landmark – Kingsley House

We strolled on the sand, on the wooden path, over the dunes, through the woods, down the sidewalk, and into the front door of our cozy home where we displayed our treasures on the kitchen table.

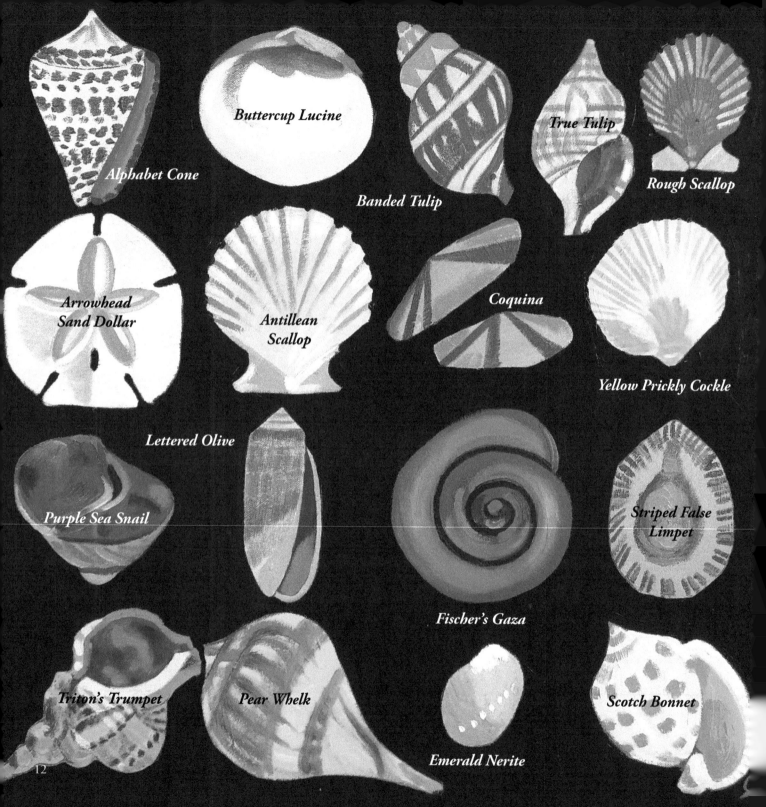

Alphabet Cone

Buttercup Lucine

Banded Tulip

True Tulip

Rough Scallop

Arrowhead
Sand Dollar

Antillean
Scallop

Coquina

Yellow Prickly Cockle

Lettered Olive

Purple Sea Snail

Fischer's Gaza

Striped False
Limpet

Triton's Trumpet

Pear Whelk

Emerald Nerite

Scotch Bonnet

Sea Urchin

Fighting Conch

Junonia

Common Sundial

Lightning Whelk

Natica

Brown-Banded Wentletrap

Baby's Ear

Kitten Paw

Scotch Bonnet

Minor Jackknife Clams

Shark Eye

Horse Mussel

Common Jingle

Deer Cowrie

13

We ate key lime pie Amelia and I had
baked, and we polished shells.

*State Wildflower – Coreopsis
or Tick Weed*

State Pie – Key Lime Pie

14

"TWEET, TWEET." The mockingbird chirped outside the window.

State Bird – Mockingbird

State Butterfly – Zebra Longwing

State Flower – Orange Blossom

15

I dreamed of mermaid's purses…

State Freshwater Fish – Largemouth Bass

State Animal – Florida Panther

decorated with Florida creatures from the land, rivers, and sea.

State Marine Mammal – Manatee   *State Reptile – American Alligator*

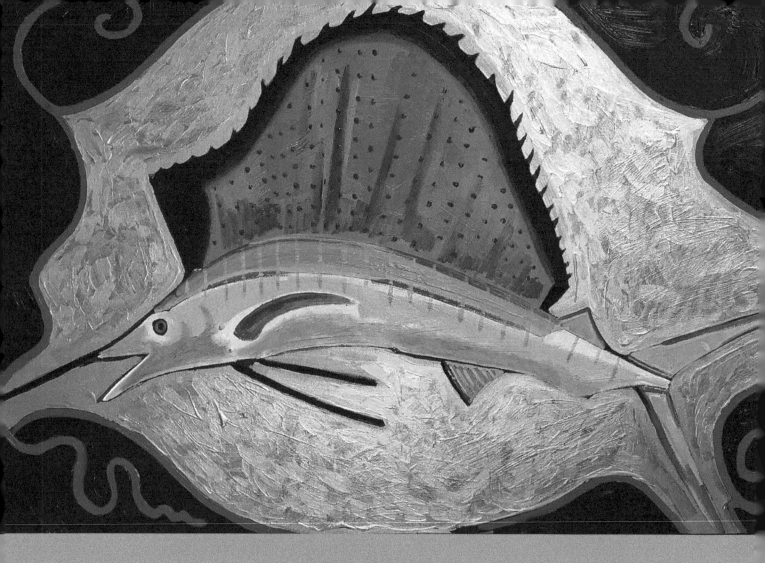

Saltwater Fish – Sailfish

Then, I worried that the mermaid was searching for her purse. I thought of a solution, so I asked, "Y'all wanna walk on back to the beach?"

So, we trekked out the front door, down the sidewalk,
through the woods, over the dunes,
on the wooden path, and onto the sand.

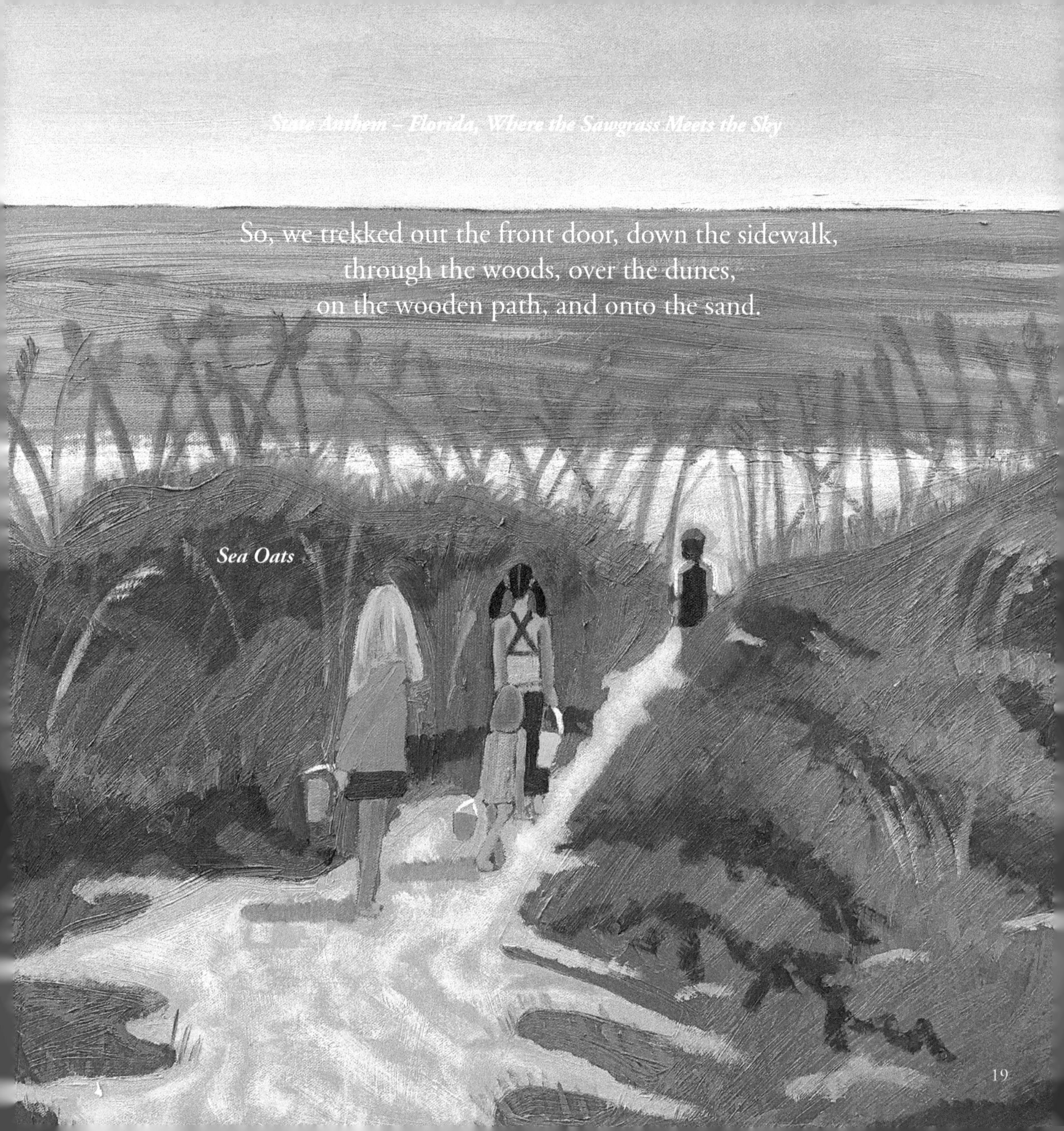

Sea Oats

19

While everyone dug for sand fleas, I made
a beeline down the beach and placed the
mermaid's purse in the perfect spot. I wrote
in the sand, *"Miss Mermaid, I found your
purse. Your friend from the land, Marjorie."*

At bedtime, Mama asked, "Any adventures today?" "I found the mermaid's purse, but I gave it back because I didn't want the mermaid to be sad," I answered. "How nice," she smiled and kissed me.

After she shut my door, I peeked through my window and spied…

Egret

the egret that perches on the tree outside my window every night.

I drifted to sleep. In my dreams, I swam through…

State Saltwater Mammal – Dolphin or Porpoise

23

an underwater world, where I spotted the mermaid!
She was cranky because she lost her purse.
But the scene changed, and the mermaid smiled…

Longsnout Seahorse

Scrawled Cowfish

State Saltwater Reptile – Loggerhead Sea Turtle

Four-Eyed Butterflyfish

Sargassum Triggerfish

French Angelfish

because she found her purse in the perfect spot. When I woke up,
I wiggled into my bikini and zipped out the front door,
down the sidewalk, through the woods, over the dunes,
on the wooden path, and onto the sand …

where I discovered a treasure box.
Inside was a ring, necklace, and letter.

State Stone –
Agatized Coral

Scallop Shell

Starfish

26

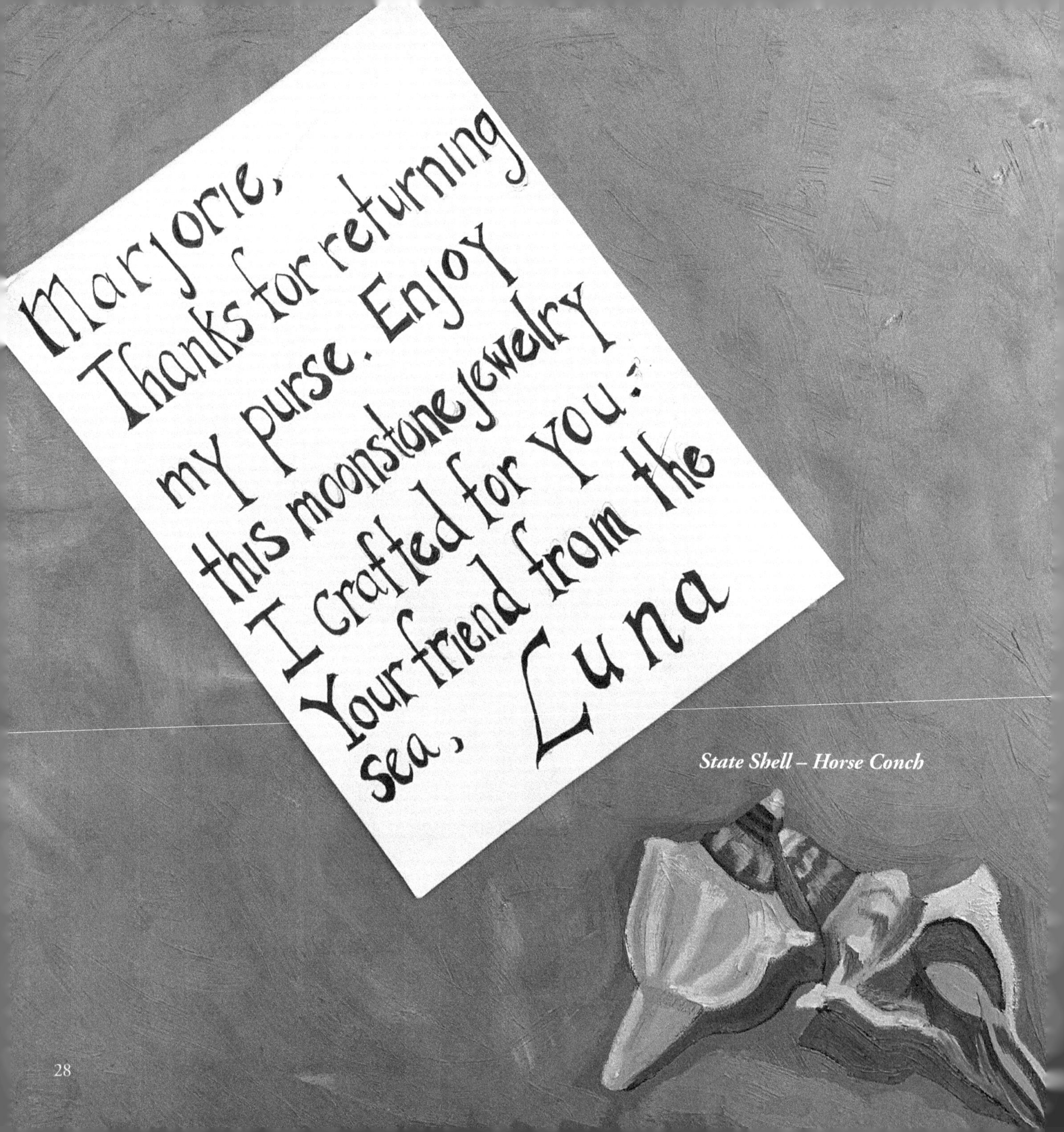

Marjorie,
Thanks for returning
my purse. Enjoy
this moonstone jewelry
I crafted for you.
Your friend from the
sea, Luna

State Shell – Horse Conch

28

State Gem – Moonstone

Parrot Fish

A mermaid's purse is the egg case for skates and some sharks. When the baby is ready, it hatches and swims away, looking like a little version of its parents. The cases are often washed up on beaches after the baby has hatched.

Luna

31

Great Blue Heron

CPSIA information can be obtained
at www.ICGtesting.com
Printed in the USA
LVHW021643100221
678898LV00009B/775